E
Cu

Curious George at the airport

MEDIALOG
Alexandria, Ky 41001

Eau Claire District Library

Curious George®
AT THE AIRPORT

Adapted from the Curious George film series
edited by Margret Rey and Alan J. Shalleck

1 9 8 7

Houghton Mifflin Company, Boston

Library of Congress Cataloging-in-Publication Data

Curious George at the airport.

"Adapted from the Curious George film series."
Summary: Curious George goes to the airport with
his friend and manages to get lost.
[1. Monkeys—Fiction.   2. Airports—Fiction]
I. Rey, Margret.   II. Shalleck, Alan J.   III. Curious
George at the airport (Motion picture)
PZ7.C92126 1987   [E]   87-3028
ISBN 0-395-45355-0

Copyright © 1987 by Houghton Mifflin Company and Curgeo Agencies, Inc.

Printed in the United States of America.

Y 10 9 8 7 6 5 4 3 2 1

"A friend of mine is flying from Africa to see us,"
said the man with the yellow hat.
"Let's go meet him at the airport."

The parking lot at the airport was full,
but George and his friend finally found
an empty place.

"Let's remember where we parked, George,
so we don't get lost when we come back."

Inside the airport,
many people were rushing around.

"Follow me and don't get lost, George,"
said the man. "We're going to meet my friend
by the luggage area."

People were crowding around the moving belt
to pick up their bags.

George was curious.
Where did the belt go?
He wanted to find out.

He jumped on.
The belt carried George through a little door

and outside to the back of the building.

Workers were loading luggage onto the belt.
They didn't see George.

He rode by them and
jumped onto another moving belt.

Now where was he?
And how would he get back to his friend?

George was scared.
Was he lost?

He got up and ran down a long hall.

Finally, George came to a door.

He opened the door and found himself
on the top floor of the airport.

From up here, George could see everything!

Then, he thought he saw a man in a yellow hat
getting off an airplane.

Could he have found his friend?

A girl who was standing nearby asked,
"Are you looking for someone?"

"Here — you can look through my binoculars.
They make things look bigger."

George looked through the binoculars.
The man in the yellow hat was someone else!

George didn't know if he would ever
find his friend.

"Don't worry," said the girl.
"I'll help you."

The girl led George downstairs and past
a sign that said, "This way to Lost and Found."

And there, inside, was his friend.
"There you are, George!" he shouted.
"I have someone I'd like you to meet."

What a surprise —
it was the man in the *other* yellow hat!

"My friend has had a long trip, George.
Let's take him home so he can rest.
How would you like to lead the way?"

And George knew just how to
get back to the car.

The three of them got into the little blue car
and went home.